I0890470

SERVICE LEARNING FOR TEENS™

IMPROVING COMMUNITY HEALTH AND SAFETY THROUGH SERVICE LEARNING

ERIN STALEY

ROSEN PUBLISHING®

New York

Published in 2015 by The Rosen Publishing Group, Inc.
29 East 21st Street, New York, NY 10010

Copyright © 2015 by The Rosen Publishing Group, Inc.

First Edition

All rights reserved. No part of this book may be reproduced in any form without permission in writing from the publisher, except by a reviewer.

Library of Congress Cataloging-in-Publication Data

Staley, Erin.
Improving community health and safety through service learning/
Erin Staley.—First edition.
pages cm.—(Service learning for teens)
Audience: Grades 7–12.
Includes bibliographical references and index.
ISBN 978-1-4777-7955-2 (library bound)
1. Service learning—Juvenile literature. 2. Social action—Juvenile literature. 3. Health—Juvenile literature. 4. Safety education—Juvenile literature. 5. Safety—Juvenile literature. I. Title.
LC220.5.S69 2014
361.3'7–dc23

2014012404

Manufactured in the United States of America

CONTENTS

INTRODUCTION

It has never been easier for today's youth to jump into community improvement. From clothing donations to animal advocacy, kindergarten through twelfth graders (K–12) and college-aged students can play an active role in volunteer projects, both great and small. One of the most rewarding "get in and give" opportunities is that of service learning. According to the National Service-Learning Clearinghouse, this concept is defined as "a teaching and learning strategy that integrates meaningful community service with instruction and reflection to enrich the learning experience, teach civic responsibility, and strengthen communities." The National Youth Leadership Council breaks it down into this analogy: "Picking up trash by a riverbank is service. Studying water samples under a microscope is learning. When students collect and analyze water samples and the local pollution control agency uses the findings to clean up a river... that is service learning."

Across the United States and in Canada, churches, community organizations, and school systems have embraced the service-learning movement. The personal and academic benefits are simply too good to overlook: enhanced education, greater confidence, improved interpersonal skills, and

During a special Earth Day cleanup event, volunteers gather in Minneapolis, Minnesota, to clean up the banks of the Mississippi River.

a heightened sense of civic responsibility. Plus, the people living in the area get to enjoy a higher quality of life. Teachers and school administrators are especially eager to tie a specific community matter into classroom curriculum. Math, science, health, English, foreign culture, art, history, and technology—these subjects can all be a part of the service-learning experience. Students are then encouraged to analyze, solve, and reflect on real-life issues and solutions. Take, for instance, a science class that offers a waste management series. A three-month string of discussion covering recycling, composting, and hazardous waste could be offered to a new residential area. Throughout the process, the science class could reflect on their participation through journaling exercises and group discussions. Another example could be a physical education class that reaches out to a women's and children's center. The participating service-learning students could construct a six-week lesson plan teaching the basics of self-defense. At the end of the term, a student demonstration would show a mastery of learned skills and offer a time to reflect on the appreciation of empowering others to stay safe.

In this book, we'll continue to define service learning as it applies to improving the health and safety of your friends, family, neighbors, and environment. We'll also take a look at examples that student groups of all ages have done to devote their time and talents to a variety of initiatives. You'll be inspired by their stories, and you'll recognize the personal benefits you'll receive from your participation. Whether you want to forge ahead with higher learning, build a successful career, travel the world, raise a family, or all of the above—your participation in a service-learning project will give you the building blocks to take on any challenge and become a productive and caring community member.

CHAPTER ONE

BEYOND THE CLASSROOM

Welcome to the wonderful world of service learning! If you're a student who wants to get involved in his or her community—to roll up your sleeves and make your community a better place to live, grow, and learn—then this educational adventure is for you. According to the National Youth Leadership Council (NYLC), service learning is "a philosophy, pedagogy, and model for community development that is used as an instructional strategy to meet learning goals and/or content standards." Practically speaking, service learning takes education beyond the classroom. It connects classroom curriculum with real-world experiences, giving students of all ages a chance to put "theory into action."

Examples of service-learning projects can include an elementary class that organizes an anti-bullying awareness marathon or a middle school physical education class that teaches expressive movement to children with developmental issues. Naturally, these classroom-related projects are woven into the students' regular classroom

Service learning is not just for impressing college recruiters or job selection committee members. It's about connecting personally, socially, and educationally with others.

schedules. The same holds true for service-learning high school and college-aged scholars. Despite their normal curriculum, they could have a specific class that gets involved in the community. For instance, a high school health class may work with a local health clinic for low-income families. Or a university marketing class may develop promotional material for a nonprofit campaign.

FOUR CATEGORIES OF SERVICE LEARNING

The Florida Department of Education and Florida Campus Compact divides service learning into four categories: direct, indirect, advocacy, and research. Direct focuses on face-to-face projects such as tutoring, peer mediation, or working with the elderly. Indirect service learning includes food and clothing drives as well as community restoration and environmental repair projects. Advocacy is all about spreading awareness. Students write, speak, teach, and present information regarding health, safety, anti-violence, and prevention. Research service learning focuses on data collection such as studies, surveys, experiments, interviews, and evaluations.

Hundreds of "Make a Difference Day" volunteers in California perform indoor and outdoor tasks to help local seniors. Willie Mae Ivory is pictured trying out her new wheelchair ramp.

This data is then used for public interest topics such as water treatments, flora and fauna studies, and residential and commercial energy audits.

THE NUTS AND BOLTS OF SERVICE LEARNING

There are many nuts and bolts to a successful service-learning project. With the assistance of faculty members, youngsters work as a team to create the program from scratch. They determine the who, what, when, where, why, and how of the project. Once the program is up and running, students take time to reflect on the experience. This can be done through journal writing or classroom discussions. Resources fromthe school as well as from the community and national groups often aid in the organization and implementation of these projects.

Reflection allows students to evaluate their emotions and experiences during service-learning projects. They can observe personal and social growth as well as learn from mistakes and challenges.

PROJECT IGNITION: CHANGING TEEN DRIVER BEHAVIOR

Car crashes are the number-one cause of death of teens in the United States. Across the country, 36 percent of teenage deaths occur in motor vehicle crashes, but Project Ignition, the NYLC's teen driver safety program, is working to bring this number to zero. Since 1983, youth leaders have partnered with teachers and communities to create the "peer-led service-learning" Project Ignition campaign. Their mission? To inspire teen driver safety in the United States and Canada. Today, Project Ignition empowers young people to proactively change teen behaviors and encourage safe driver behavior. They do this by organizing events, demonstrations, and announcements. Kelita Svoboda Bak, NYLC's chief executive officer, elaborates on the program's official website, nylc.org:

> From changing laws by working with state legislators, to hosting awareness-raising events in their local communities, teens are saving lives and changing the way their friends think about safe, responsible driving. Each year we look forward to seeing all of the impactful, innovative ways that youth use their voice and creativity to lead campaigns that tackle driving safety through Project Ignition, and each year these passionate young people continue to exceed our expectations.

Project Ignition is able to maintain its programs thanks to $2,000 per-school grants. American and Canadian public and private high schools can apply, but only twenty-five schools are selected each year. Once awarded, the campaigns can move into full swing. Teens engage their peers in an impactful awareness campaign the following school year. Direct support—personal support, trainings, and online resources—is given to adult mentors and student teams through the Generator School Network. This sets them up for success long after the grant money is spent. The ten best school campaigns are then awarded an additional $7,500 each to continue as Project Ignition National Leader Schools.

Distraction.gov reports that "a quarter of teens respond to a text message once or more every time they drive." Twenty percent admit they have "extended, multi-message text conversations while driving."

SERVICE LEARNING: A WIN-WIN

Service learning is a win-win for classes, faculty, schools, and the community. Because students are engaged intellectually, emotionally, socially, and physically, they develop a sense of ownership. For example, if a high school English class were to design a reading program for visually impaired community members, the participating students would develop the long-term agenda. It would be their responsibility to select the reading material, prepare the venue, determine who would read, and who would advertise the event. On each reading day, students would need to arrive early enough to set up the room, get any sound equipment in running order, and welcome visitors.

As the program continued throughout the term, hiccups would be inevitable. Maybe the group would find the reading selections to be dull, or maybe the designated reader was home in bed because of a nasty cold. The service-learning group members would need to think on their feet in order to solve problems. They would need to brainstorm a solution, make the necessary adjustments, and forge ahead to reach their goals. This requires critical-thinking and interpersonal skills, which produce self-esteem and confidence. Respect, friendship, compassion, and acceptance would blossom.

From an academic point of view, the service-learning youths would experience a greater understanding of their course content, both English and literature. They would also gather valuable insights into possible career options such as education, health and safety, and public speaking. Often, service-learning experiences attract the attention of university admissions personnel and potential employers. Last, but certainly not least, service learning enforces the idea that students are global citizens. Their thoughts, behaviors, and actions affect those around them, whether they know it or not; and they learn that a conscientious effort will foster global awareness and change a community, nation, or world for the better.

Service learning has far-reaching benefits for faculty and schools, too. Teachers and counselors who advise on these projects are invigorated by their students' enthusiasm to help, learn, and grow. Teaching and counseling methods are fine-tuned as faculty members discover what grips the attention of their students. Plus, they enjoy the satisfaction of knowing they're a part of something bigger than themselves. Schools enjoy a rich connection with the public, and community members can contribute to the educational process of future generations.

A PEEK INTO THE HISTORY OF SERVICE LEARNING

As we go back through the pages of American history, we discover that community service learning was an integral part of campus life during the nineteenth century. Sororities, fraternities, and campus faith-based groups in colleges and universities expected

American philosopher John Dewey (1859–1952) campaigned for experiential education. This teaching method focuses on the personal experiences of the learner rather than the learning gained from texts and lectures.

their students to get involved with civic projects. In the early twentieth century, philosopher and educator John Dewey (1859–1952) championed his belief that public education should produce respectable citizens. Despite gender, ethnicity, race, or economic status, students could unite to find solutions to common issues. Three decades later, President Franklin D. Roosevelt introduced the Civilian Conservation Corps. Its purpose was to revitalize the nation after the Great Depression (1929 to the early 1940s). Thousands of unemployed men, namely seventeen and eighteen year olds, joined this peacetime army from 1933 to 1942. These men were commissioned to lessen the destruction and erosion of the nation's natural resources. During this time, they received academic, vocational, and on-the-job training. By the end of the program in 1942, three million young men had benefitted from their participation with the Corps.

Service learning reached a new level when President Roosevelt signed the Servicemen's Readjustment Act of 1944. Commonly referred to as the G.I. Bill of Rights, this bill linked service with education for military volunteers. In exchange for their military service, educational opportunities would be granted. But it wasn't until the late 1960s that the term "service learning" caught on as a catchphrase. It was used by educators Robert Sigmon and William Ramsey, who played an active role in the Southern Regional Education Board conference in Atlanta, Georgia. They needed to name the future service-learning program, and they tried many different names—action learning, experience learning, experiential learning, and work learning—until they finally decided to call it service learning. It was the word "service" that gave the phrase a value and an attitude. When the two words are put together—service and learning—the discipline of learning and active reflection are implied. Service learning is not merely academic or casual learning, but real, hands-on service.

The Southern Regional Education Board conference was planned to discuss the pros and cons of service-learning programs on the campuses of America's secondary education institutions. In attendance were sponsors from the Atlanta Urban Corps, City of Atlanta, Peace Corps, Regional Education Board, and U.S. Department of Health, Education, and Welfare. After much discussion, they determined that colleges and universities should encourage their students to participate in service-learning scenarios. Funds would be provided, and students, faculty, and private agency officials would to work together to plan and implement the programs. In addition, academic learning would be woven throughout the experience.

Fast forward to the 1980s, and a college-wide service-learning network was created: the National Campus Compact. Today, over 1,100 college and university presidents continue to advocate the civic purposes of higher education. Soon, President George H. W. Bush passed the National and Community Service Act of 1990. This act sanctioned various full- or part-time programs to fight against illiteracy and poverty, provide new educational and work skills, and satisfy environmental needs. President William J. Clinton approved the National and Community Service Trust Act of 1993. Its goal was to offer service opportunities to all Americans, despite their age or background. Under the act's umbrella was a program called Learn and Serve America (LSA). Today, LSA is the country's largest funder of service-learning programs. LSA provides grants to elementary through high school programs as well as to community groups and higher education institutions with service-learning projects. It also provides research, how-to's, curricula, program models, training, and technical assistance to schools, faculty, and parents. Since then, the popularity of service learning has skyrocketed across the United States and Canada.

CHAPTER TWO

CREATING RIPPLES

While there are many service-learning categories in which students can get involved, one of the most popular—and needed—is that of health and safety. From social work to preventative care, and from occupational therapy to medicine, students of health and safety can have a direct impact on the well-being of their friends, family, and neighbors. It's all about finding an urgent need, and then figuring out a solution that will create many ripples within your community.

STUDENTS HELPING STUDENTS

A popular service-learning experience among students is a project geared toward helping fellow students. In the areas of health and safety, this could mean presenting tips on injury prevention at home, revealing nutritional food options to combat childhood obesity, or developing a safe-sex awareness program. One such initiative was created by students who were so

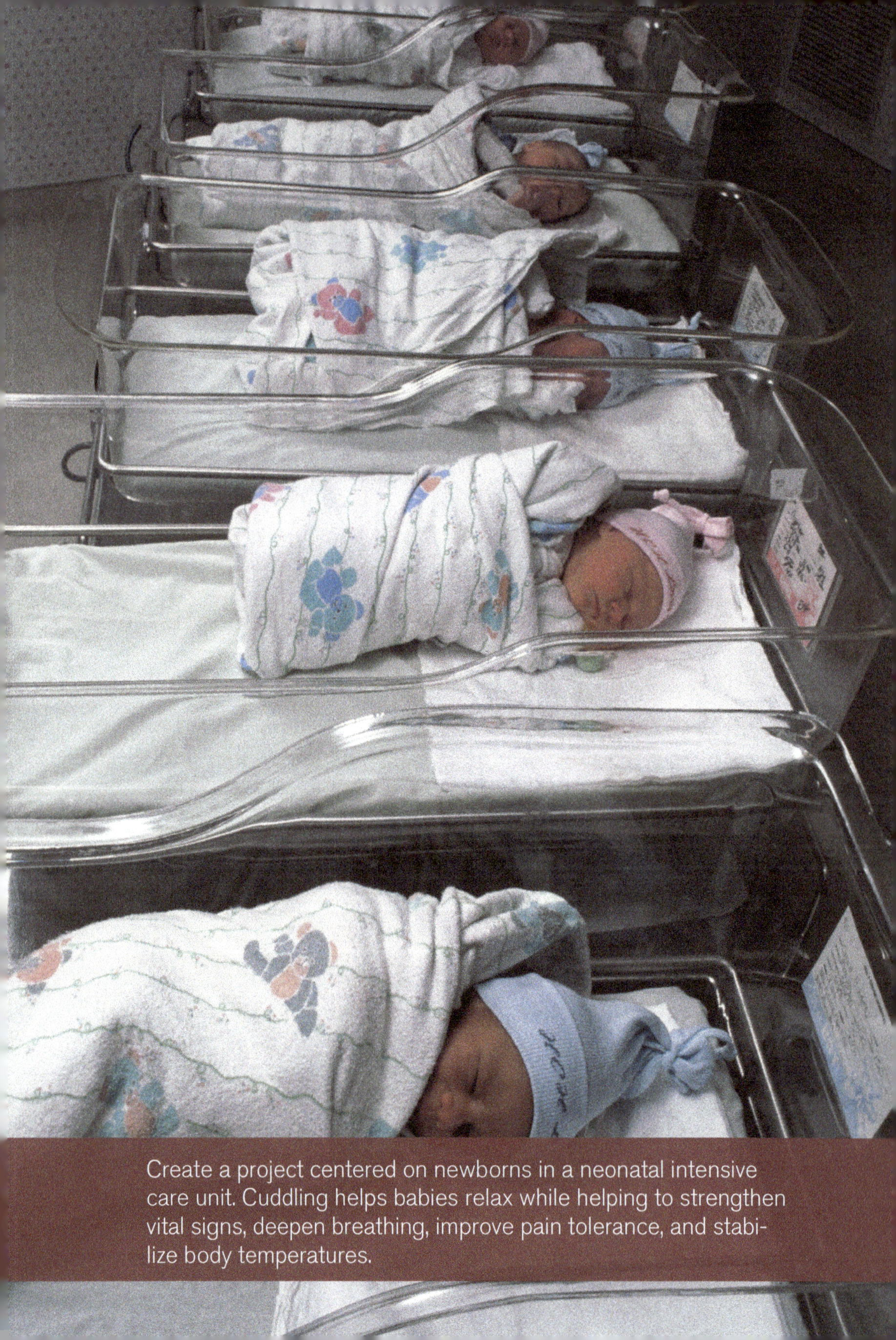

Create a project centered on newborns in a neonatal intensive care unit. Cuddling helps babies relax while helping to strengthen vital signs, deepen breathing, improve pain tolerance, and stabilize body temperatures.

touched by a crisis in their community that they created "Blankets, Babies, and HIV/AIDS Awareness." Too many babies were suffering from severe damage to their immune systems as a result of HIV (human immunodeficiency virus) and AIDS (acquired immunodeficiency syndrome). The students came up with a brilliant idea to make quilt-like baby blankets. They borrowed traditional geometric patterns used by pioneer women and purchased soft fabric in soothing colors to create these comfort-giving blankets. A parent volunteer helped to sew the seams. Once the blankets were completed, the students took them on a tour, teaching their peers about HIV/AIDS. The blankets were used as a visual aid and were eventually donated to a local organization that cared for babies living with HIV/AIDS.

Another health and safety example is that of Karen Lefave's third-grade class at Brayton Elementary School in North Adams, Massachusetts. "Bullying on the bus set the tone for the whole day and often left my third graders in tears," she tells Pamela Roberts of Responsive Classroom. Lefave's students felt powerless against the yelling, swearing, pushing, and vandalizing bullies who rode their school buses. Some of the third graders reported stomachaches, while others had trouble settling down during class time. Bullying was a real problem until Lefave applied the community service-learning (CSL) concept to the problem. She enlisted the help of school adjustment counselor Nancy Gallagher, and together, they helped the third graders face their concerns through discussions, drawings, and stories.

During this process, the children discovered that the fifth graders were the main culprits. With guidance from Lefave and Gallagher, they recruited five older students to play the role of bus mediator. During their twice-a-week language arts period, third and fifth graders discussed the effects of bullying, what it feels like to be bullied, and why bullies do what they do. In small groups—each including a fifth

Affected by bullying? Stop it in its tracks by teaming up with local and online antibullying programs. Be a part of the change that helps countless others.

grader—the students role-played bullying situations. They also came up with possible scenarios to prevent the behavior, such as confronting it, walking away, or seeking help from an adult.

In addition, Lefave's students realized that the bus drivers could become a part of the resolution. If the bullying students knew their bus drivers as well as they knew their teachers, they may be less likely to act out. As a result, Lefave's class interviewed and photographed volunteering bus drivers. They then created posters to hang throughout the school. One example read: "Meet the driver of the Flower Bus. His name is Mr. Wilson. He has a dog. He likes to travel." Additionally, the bus drivers were given a voice in passenger policy and discipline within the school community. The service-learning third graders also realized that they could improve their own behavior in order to influence change for the better. In the end, the students rewrote school policy, which was then approved by administrators. Their efforts were greatly rewarded as their buses became safer, and the number of bullying incidents was cut in half.

IN THEIR OWN BACKYARD

We've learned that service learning often takes place within schools and communities. But in the case of tenth-grade students at Humboldt Senior High School in St. Paul, Minnesota, it took place within their own backyard. Erosion was threatening the school grounds, and the teens took it upon themselves to create a project that would keep the soil intact. With the help of teachers, master gardeners, a landscape design team, the Ramsey-Washington Metro Watershed District, and the local university's Center for Global & Environmental Education, the tenth graders devised a plan. They began by securing a grant that would allow them to perform a three-part research. The Humboldt Senior High students needed to research the storm water runoff and its impact on the final destination,

Gather your friends together and develop an "In the Garden" project. You can educate others with how-to tips for growing their favorite herbs, fruits, and vegetables.

the Mississippi River. They also needed to look at the local root structure of plants. This flora would have to be strong enough to withstand erosion while increasing soil infiltration. The design team then created gardens and supervised a 140-student party to plant flowers and shrubs.

The service-learning project was a hit. According to "Student-Learning: An Implementation Guide for High School Teachers," advising teacher Jodie Prohaska noted, "Some of the students who aren't always engaged in the classroom participated fully in the project, and then experienced such a feeling of success when the planting took place."

A SCHOOL-WIDE QUEST

Three hundred Quest Early College High School students in Humble, Texas, set out to serve an entire community with their multi-dimensional service-learning projects. Throughout the school year, they reserved one day a week to put their school's outreach philosophy into action. Quest is a progressive school that believes service-learning opportunities increase students' engagement and motivation to learn. In the faculty's opinion, students enjoy a greater learning experience when they master a lesson rather than earn a grade. It is the true essence of learning; and it is this philosophy that is put into action during the school's weekly service-learning lesson plan.

Each Friday during the academic year, Quest students were divided into groups to work at various service-learning sites. These included local elementary schools,

Theoretical concepts taught in the classroom come to life when students get involved in helping others—even four-legged creatures both big and small.

a hospital clinic, a nursing home, a center for disabled young adults, and an animal shelter. One group, called the "Green Team," consisted of environmental stewards who cared for a collection of small forests just twenty miles from Quest Early College High School. Another group pretended to be early settlers. The females dressed in long skirts, and the males donned britches. Together, they gave touring elementary students a peek into the life of a nineteenth-century pioneer farm replica that had been built by previous Quest students.

At the end of the term, all of the participating Quest students wrote reflections. They talked about the excitement of getting ready to help others, the challenges they faced, and the feelings they had as they made an impact on the lives of others. Even the teachers noticed a change in their students. Each student expressed an improved air of confidence, responsibility, patience, initiative, and sense of purpose. The teachers could

BOZEMAN'S COFFEE 2 COMPOST PROGRAM

If you like coffee, then you'll love what Coffee 2 Compost (C2C) does with its spent grounds! Students in Bozeman, Montana, cruise city streets on bicycles outfitted with trailers to collect donations from local coffee shops. They bring thousands of pounds of these environmentally valuable leftovers—which are loaded with organic resources—to compost bins in the area. According to "Coffee 2 Compost In a Nutshell," which was published on 1000newgardens.ning.com:

> ...Used coffee grounds are a great source of nitrogen microorganisms that decompose organic matter. Once the beans go through the brewing process, most of their acidity goes into your cup, and what is left is a fairly neutral bacteria population promoting substance. Coffee shops brew an incredible amount of grounds every day, and by organizing their transport, we [the C2C program volunteers] assist shops seeking to positively impact the local environment, contribute nutrients to local agriculture, and save some space in those huge blue dumpsters that line alleyways. Many shops end up decreasing the size of their waste receptacles, therefore saving some money on that monthly bill!

Volunteers estimate that the C2C program has prevented five thousand pounds of coffee waste from being

(continued on the next page)

(continued from the previous page)

sent to landfills each year. Plus, the program educates community youngsters on the science of composting and looking for creative ways to cycle nutrients through a community while maintaining food security. C2C has been a great success, so much so that program coordinators have created a handbook to help others start C2C programs in their own communities.

tell that each participating teen felt valued, and recognition between social and emotional learning had been made thanks to service learning. One Quest student tells Barbara Cervone of whatkidscando.org, "It's the little stone that creates a huge ripple." Another Quest student agreed by saying:

> You get to learn so much about yourself, you grow so much patience, you learn to see the world through another person's eyes. Now I can actually explain a concept up here [the head] to a child who could only grasp something down there [the heart].

SENIOR GAMES

Often, creating ripples with service-learning initiatives can be fun! Ivy Tech Community College, an accredited community college in Indiana known for a long-standing tradition of education excellence, has figured out how to offer a wealth of volunteer and service-learning

Looking for project ideas? Create a senior-citizens program. Implement an exercise course. Teach basic computer skills. Deliver hot meals. You may just make a friend while learning something new.

opportunities *and* keep the learning exciting. Its Bloomington campus teams up with community partners, such as Area 10 Agency on Aging. This nonprofit organization provides housing, meal delivery, bus service, and volunteer opportunities to senior citizens. One of Area 10's programs is "Senior Games," an annual event designed to promote active and healthy aging. Senior citizens come out to compete in a friendly game of pool, horseshoes, golf, Texas Hold 'Em poker, and "Senior Squabble," their take on a televised game show. The Ivy Tech nursing students make sure everyone is having a good time, staying safe and active, and enjoying a day of fun learning. And for an added bonus, this day of play is all a part of their nursing curriculum during the academic year.

In addition to working with the elderly, Ivy Tech nursing students organize cultural fairs, teach first aid to elementary classes, share nutrition tips with Girl Scout troops, and build therapy tables for students with disabilities. Former Chancellor John Whikehart is quoted in *Ivy Tech Community College Bloomington News* as saying, "…Through volunteerism and service learning, Ivy Tech-Bloomington has contributed a total value of $1,185,995 [a figure based on independentsector.org's national value of volunteer time] in the communities we serve [in a year's time]." Thanks to this Indiana community college, many ripples were created, as well as a whole lot of fun!

CHAPTER THREE

SERVICE LEARNING BEYOND YOUR BORDERS

There are a great number of North American colleges and universities that give their graduates and undergraduates an opportunity to jump into service learning abroad. Students can visit a remote region of the world, bringing with them medical supplies, technology, and much-needed know-how. While abroad, students learn and earn, gaining academic credit by collaborating with foreign communities to solve pressing health and safety issues. This experience offers complete immersion, a method of turning the world into a classroom.

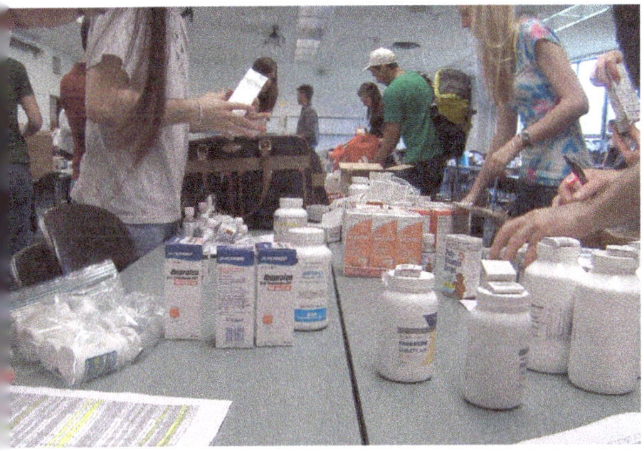

Michigan State University student volunteers process approximately $100,000 in donated medical supplies for a ten-day orthopedic health mission in Trujillo, a coastal city in northwestern Peru.

GLOBAL YOUTH SERVICE DAY

Millions of youth in more than 135 countries come together each April to celebrate Global Youth Service Day (GYSD), a worldwide Youth Service America (YSA) campaign honoring student-led service-learning projects. GYSD is all about changing the world through service and inspiring young people—just like you—to get involved in a meaningful way. They encourage service on a national and international level while providing funding, tips, tools, and training to maximize the quality and impact of service-learning projects.

The GYSD website offers three ways to celebrate Global Youth Service Day. First, you can "Host a Celebration Event" by thanking the youth who have served throughout the year with a particular event. This could be in the form of a community, town council, or school board meeting. It could also be a party where you present awards to youth volunteers. Second, you could "Engage Media" by publicly thanking the many people who helped to make your service-learning project so successful. This can be done in a school or community newspaper, through social media posts, or on television in a news report or interview. Finally, you can "Advocate on Behalf of Youth" by calling on local organizations to join youth service or service-learning programs. This could be a class, faith-based group, or club such as the 4-H, Girl and Boy Scouts, Boys and Girls Clubs of America, Big Brothers Big Sisters of America, or the National FFA Organization. If you need additional ideas, gysd.org has a number of resources to help you get started.

Rutgers University in New Brunswick, New Jersey, is one higher-education institution that offers this type of educational experience. Students can select from a menu of International Service Learning (ISL) destinations to find an area of interest. Options range from language education in Argentina, agricultural studies in Turkey, health clinics in Cuba, and urban poverty assistance in Greece.

BECOME A PART OF THE SOLUTION WITH INTERNATIONAL SERVICE LEARNING

International Service Learning (ISL) is an organization that sends over two thousand college and university students to more than a dozen developing countries each year. ISL's mission is to provide health care treatments, supplies, and services to those in need. ISL got its start in 1994, when Michael Birnbaum, who would later found ISL, toured the banana industry in Central America's Costa Rica. The banana plantation workforce was comprised of Nicaraguan refugees who lived in makeshift tents made of plastic sheets and bamboo poles. When a skirmish between the plantation owners and workers broke out, vengeful plantation owners decided to teach their workforce a lesson by bulldozing a section of temporary housing. Workers had no choice but to rebuild their housing, especially as the women and children needed to be protected

Health and safety service-learning projects are known for raising public awareness. This is especially true when working in other lands, including the banana farms in Costa Rica *(pictured)*.

from threatening rains. As they slowly began to rebuild what had been destroyed, a bus carrying touring American college students approached. A few dozen students exited the bus and began taking pictures of the commotion. But when asked to help—even for an hour or two—they declined, boarded the bus, and left. Birnbaum wondered how many women and children were left sleeping in the heavy rains that night.

Inspired, Birnbaum set out to organize what the ISL website calls "student study tours with a meaningful and challenging service component—to combine adventure, service, and learning." Today, ISL sends students from more than one hundred American and Canadian colleges and universities—ranging from small private schools to large institutions—to travel, learn, and offer vital services to people dealing with often tragic situations in Africa, Mexico, the Caribbean, and Central and South America. ISL participants are active in repairing homes and community buildings, providing know-how, and transporting supplies such as appliances, mobile dental equipment, and vehicles. ISL is proud of its programs because they are safe, dynamic, and life changing for the people in need, the participants, and the world.

Communities such as this one in Georgia benefit when young people get involved. Students offer insightful ideas as well as enthusiasm to "pick up a hammer" and get involved.

MARYMOUNT SHARES HELPING HANDS

Like Rutgers, Marymount University in Arlington, Virginia, partnered with ISL. In 2011 the university arranged for a two-week Physical Therapy Clinical Practicum II course at the Manos Abiertas (Spanish for "open hands") orphanage in Costa Rica. Twenty-five third-year Doctor of Physical Therapy (D.P.T.) candidates signed up to care for the orphanage's residents, who suffered from severe neurological and musculoskeletal disorders.

The Marymount University D.P.T. students took time to academically prepare themselves for this highly anticipated experience. They took a Spanish-language course in order to better communicate with the orphanage's residents and staff. They also fulfilled community service projects, such as fitness screenings, that would later be modified for the Costa Rican patients. Finally, the D.P.T. students performed residential rehabilitation facility clinical rotations to refine their physical therapy treatment skills for the care of the Manos Abiertas children. In addition to academic preparations, each D.P.T. student took on a leadership role in the physical arrangements. Some got involved in fundraising efforts, while others collected medical supplies such as wheelchairs, crutches, walkers, ultrasound units, and braces.

Even with their preparations and the warm welcome of Manos Abiertas, the Marymount students weren't completely prepared for what they would find on their first visit. Despite the clean, well-maintained, and kind oversight the *hermanas* (Spanish meaning "sisters") had for the children in their care, the severity of their physical issues was striking. Garrett Hurd had this to share with Marymount director of public relations Laurie Callahan: "My stomach dropped when I saw some of the patients that I was to evaluate, their bodies locked in unnatural positions, painfully contorted and twisted... Then something incredible happened. Slowly but steadily, my education began to kick in." Hurd and the rest of the D.P.T. students got busy doing what they do best: helping patients regain their physical agility. By the second day, progress was already being made, and the students were encouraged to keep going.

But it wasn't smooth sailing for the entire stay. Thanks to customs issues and postponed flights, the planned shipment of medical supplies was delayed. The D.P.T. candidates had to think outside of the box. Their patients were depending on them for care. Their solution was to repair and customize the on-site equipment to meet each patient's need. Even if it meant piecing together parts from broken down wheelchairs, D.P.T. candidates were determined to figure out how to make it work for their new friends. This experience taught the Marymount students that the latest medical equipment isn't always necessary for successful outcomes. Sometimes a footrest made out of foam and duct tape really does make all the difference to one's recovery. Eventually, the supplies did arrive, nearly two weeks later and just before their departure day.

In addition to their Manos Abiertas work, the Marymount D.P.T. candidates hosted a health and wellness event for two underprivileged neighborhoods, where they went from door to door and provided a basic health screening. Those residents who needed additional attention were invited to a health fair the following day, where the students performed injury, range of motion, balance, strength, aerobic capacity, and nutrition evaluations. At first, the locals were nervous and unwilling to talk to the D.P.T. students.

But when balloon animals appeared on the scene, the little ones swarmed in to play. The ice was broken, and the students were able to help with treatment plans and how-to tips to handle a broad range of physical challenges. In the end, the students knew they had lifted the spirits of the community, and they were convinced that happiness could grow out of dire circumstances.

NBA player Tyler Zeller *(left)* looks on during an NBA fitness clinic for Harlem youth at the Children's Aid Society Dunlevy Milbank Boys & Girls Club.

During the reflection process, the Marymount D.P.T. students experienced life- and career-changing situations. Katie Kavanagh was one such student. She tells Callahan, "The patients we had the privilege to work with in Costa Rica helped us more than we helped them. I am so grateful to have had this experience." Fellow classmate Pam Jennings agreed: "This practicum forced me outside of my comfort zone, which helped me to grow as a practitioner. It also opened my eyes to a different way of living and made me realize how blessed I am to have everything that has been provided in my life." Even the accompanying physical therapy faculty weighed in. Dr. Diana Venskus recalls:

> As we prepared to leave, Sister Marlene Rodriquez, the founder of Manos Abiertas and Corazón Redentor and superior of the religious community there, told me that our students had done more in fifteen days than any other person or group had done in fifteen years to advance physical-therapy care for their residents!

That's the power of service learning, especially beyond your borders.

CHAPTER FOUR
HITTING CLOSE TO HOME

Many health and safety service-learning programs hit close to home and affect us, our health, and our environment. This is especially true when it comes to our food, including the way it is grown and packaged for distribution. America's first president, George Washington, recognized the greatness of this phenomenon when he said: "Agriculture is the most healthful, most useful, and most noble employment of man." Why did Washington feel so strongly? Because agriculture produces the food and home products that keep us alive and well. And to champion sound agricultural practices among America's youth, the Future Farmers of America (FFA) was founded in 1928. Its purpose is "to make a positive difference in the lives of students by developing their potential for premier leadership, personal growth,

Warren High School FFA president Brandon Lane *(left)* and vice president Ashley Payne roll up their sleeves to shovel corn as part of a service-learning project in Marietta, Ohio.

and career success through agricultural education." The FFA maintained this philosophy even after their 1988 name change to the National FFA Organization. It also extended its chapters to Puerto Rico and the United States Virgin Islands. National FFA Organization chief executive officer Dr. Dwight Armstrong had this to say, as noted by nationalffa.wordpress.com:

> FFA is preparing our youth to ensure the security of our country's food, fiber, and natural resources for years to come. Through real-world experiences, the nation's agricultural teachers are helping students develop the technical knowledge, skills, and problem-solving capabilities to be the industry's leaders of tomorrow. FFA members will be tomorrow's advocates for agriculture.

With the motto "Learning to Do, Doing to Learn, Earning to Live, Living to Serve," the National FFA Organization advocates for service learning. Each member—middle school through college-aged students—must be enrolled in an agriculture class. This can include, but is not limited to, animal and plant science, horticulture, and agriculture mechanics. From there, the FFA gives youngsters hands-on learning experiences with activities both inside and outside of the classroom. Theirs is a "three-circle model of education" that shapes student-led programs: classroom instruction, hands-on learning, and leadership development. Today, the FFA's reach extends far beyond the agriculture industry by preparing students for more than three hundred careers in science and business, as well as in food safety, security, and production.

FOOD FOR ALL

The world's population is growing. In fact, a 2013 United Nations report noted, "The current world population of 7.2 billion is projected to increase by 1 billion over the next twelve years and reach 9.6 billion by 2050." These statistics reflect an ongoing demand for food, sustainability, and agriculture know-how, which is crucial to feeding the world's rising population. The agriculture industry and National FFA Organization recognized this need a long time ago. Together, they set out to unite skilled, educated, and passionate people who were dedicated to feeding future generations. This lofty goal meant teaching students how to raise chickens and provide fresh meat and eggs, while educating the community on sustainable food practices, such as container and backyard gardening.

In 2013, the FFA was awarded more than $320,000 in grant money—sponsored by Farmers Feeding the World and the Howard G. Buffett Foundation—for their Food For All program. This grant money was distributed among FFA chapters across the country to sustain their year-long student-initiated programs to address local hunger needs. FFA chapters could apply for up to $2,500 in grant money for already established or brand-new anti-hunger service-learning initiatives. This program still exists today. FFA members are encouraged not only to provide food for local residents in need, but also to develop community gardens to supplement their school or local food pantry. FFA members are a part of every stage of the FFA: Food For All Project adventure, and they stay connected through updates, accomplishment reports, and an online project reflection survey.

One way they do this is by providing funds through the FFA: Food For All program.

IT'S IN THE BAG!

In 2012, the small community of Ridgemont had the highest obesity rates in Ohio. It also held the highest obesity rate among third graders in the county. To make matters worse, 40 percent of students qualified to receive free or reduced-priced lunches because of low family incomes. This meant that families were not always able to put food on the table, which meant that children were either malnourished or going hungry. Reliey Drum told Andrew Flinn of wktn.com, "When students are hungry in school, it really splits their attention. They aren't able to focus, all they can think about is food." Ridgemont FFA members realized how dire this situation truly was. They combined innovation and passion to combat hunger in their school district and created a service-learning solution known as the Back Pack Buddies. This innovative Ridgemont FFA program provided healthy food choices to Ridgemont Elementary students who may not have these items available at home. According to Drum, "We send a packet of food over to the elementary school for students who are on a confidential list that we get through the National School Lunch Program. It gives them food for over the weekend at the end of the month so they can eat if they have no food at home."

At the beginning of the year, thirty-five students received a lunch and dinner as well as a weekend snack. By the end of the year, sixty-five students had received the food donations. In 2013, the FFA members packed

A Noyes Elementary School second grader picks up her Back Pack Buddies bag in St. Joseph, Missouri. Thanks to a service-learning program, she has enough food for the weekend.

five hundred meals to give to seventy-five students ranging from kindergarten to third grade. Today, they are working to increase that number in order to take care of all of the hungry children in their area. But this effort requires money. Each Back Pack food pack costs $3.50 and consists of two breakfasts, two lunches, two dinners, and two snacks. A $65 donation can support one child in need for an entire school year. To cover the costs of Back Pack Buddies, FFA members have relied on donations from caring neighbors and an FFA: Food For All grant. These monies offset the food pack costs at the end of each month, but Ridgemont FFA members weren't thinking short-term. They provided "do-it-yourself" gifts, earth boxes so that families could learn how to grow their own food and fill their tables with fresh, wholesome produce. The Ridgemont FFA Back Pack Buddies program was a raving success, and it gave the students a way to exercise their academic skills. Drum explains:

> When we started the program several years ago, we did a survey with the teachers on student performance at the school. Later on, we did a follow-up survey that showed significant improvement in grades, in attendance, and improvements in their quality of participation in class. So having that last meal over the weekend has helped them in school as well.

HOME ALONE SAFETY

Many children across Canada and the United States are home alone after school. This can be scary for some youngsters, so a second-grade class in Minnesota decided to do something about it. They created the "Giving Safety Wings" project, designed to emphasize the "how" of being safe at home. Students educated themselves by reading articles and watching movies about

By getting involved in the well-being of schools, workplaces, and public environments, you and local public servants can create many ripples in your future and the future of your community.

being home alone. They learned about the poisons that many households have in their cupboards and pantries. They invited police and fire department officials to work with them in developing a list of safety rules to follow. The students then participated in role-playing by acting out possible scenarios in order to learn how to respond. They also drew these safe practices on homemade kites using cartoons. The kites flew high as the mayor gave a press conference on child safety. With this simple project, the class caught the attention of their community, empowering themselves for a lifetime.

SPREADING THE CHRISTMAS CHEER

The holiday time can be especially difficult for families. Limited funds can make it difficult to buy gifts, treat loved ones to a lavish meal, and do fun activities that make the time memorable. That is why the University of British Columbia Okanagan (UBCO) education students in Canada added a holiday twist to their version of service learning. As part of an educational art portfolio requirement, students crafted holiday cards to give to clients at Kelowna's Gospel Mission. The Connecting at Christmas initiative was affiliated with the UBCO Learning Exchange program, but it got its start when a former student-driven volunteer project connected with the homeless community. Program coordinator of the learning exchange Lori Field had this to share on the univeristy website: "A student was asked if they [sic] had a pen and paper so that one of the people could write a letter home. This request came as a surprise to the student because it was such a small thing. Yet, it is not something that homeless people have ready access to." This led to student visits. They spent time with the people at the Kelowna Gospel Mission each week and helped to get the message-filled holiday cards delivered to family and friends in time for Christmas.

From the Kelowna Gospel Mission clients to the students themselves, the response was overwhelmingly positive. One mission guest, Tom Alan Morris, expressed his appreciation for the time and effort the students put into the cards, saying, "I feel this is quite an honour to have people take time out of their day, come down here, and help me pick out a Christmas card for my friend. It's nice to have something like this to give." Veronica Cowan, Kelowna Gospel Mission's casework manager, weighed in on the project: "It's a wonderful thing—people from different backgrounds coming together to create a connection at Christmas. Having something as simple as a Christmas card really makes a difference in the lives of people in need. It is a time of caring, and the feeling of respect and hope really shines through." The students were also delighted with their contributions and will continue to spread the Christmas cheer during future holiday seasons.

SAN GABRIEL CHRISTIAN SCHOOL STUDENTS SAY "YES" TO A BETTER WORLD

In the fall of 2010, Clarence Atwater, a seventh-grade science teacher at San Gabriel Christian School in San Gabriel, California, challenged and inspired his students to engage their community in service-learning projects. His idea was to blend environmental issues with science. The result? A waste-reduction campaign at the school. Atwater's students called themselves the "YES" team, an acronym that stands for "Young Environmental Specialists." With help from the Los Angeles County Department of Public Works, the YES team toured a local recycling facility. Enthused, they encouraged their own families to use reusable shopping bags and energy saving light bulbs. The YES team even hosted an ink cartridge and unwanted cell phone collection throughout the year and jumped into other waste-reduction and recycling activities, including Nike's "Reuse a Shoe" program, which collects and repurposes used sneakers into playground equipment for low-income areas.

In January 2011, Mr. Atwater's students reached out to the community with an e-waste collection event. By working with E-Waste Center, Inc., a company that hosts e-waste collection events, Atwater's students accepted used computers and televisions from San Gabriel residents. Their efforts kept more than thirty-one thousand pounds of e-waste out of

Mobile devices contain toxic materials that enter the environment when tossed in the garbage. Instead, provide a recycling program that ensures the safe repurposing of cell phones, tablets, and laptops.

landfills. In addition, YES team members raised several thousands of dollars for eco-club funds as well as for new computer equipment, a printer, and cameras, all dog-eared for project-documentation purposes. The YES team continues to make a great impact on waste reduction and has gone on to receive local awards and recognition.

CHAPTER FIVE

YOU CAN DO IT, TOO!

By now, you're probably eager to jump into your own service-learning project. Below is a step-by-step guide to help you maximize your efforts and complete your project with flying colors. Just keep in mind that these hands-on initiatives take a lot of time and behind-the-scenes effort to be successful. You'll need to be 100 percent committed to your cause and your team in order to do this right. If you're ready to roll up your sleeves and make a health and safety difference in your life and in the lives of others, then let's get started.

FIND AND INVESTIGATE THE NEED

No doubt your community has a number of ways in which you can meet health and safety needs. But how can you determine these needs? And which one will inspire you to devote your time and energy to finding a solution? The first thing on the list is to check in with a local health care clinic. Maybe its administrators would welcome a series of community discussions regarding a variety of topics, such as healthy eating, blood drives, or the facts, figures, myths, and truths about HIV/AIDS and sexually transmitted infections. You could also connect with local utility companies and environmental groups. Perhaps they would welcome an energy saving workshop or new recycling

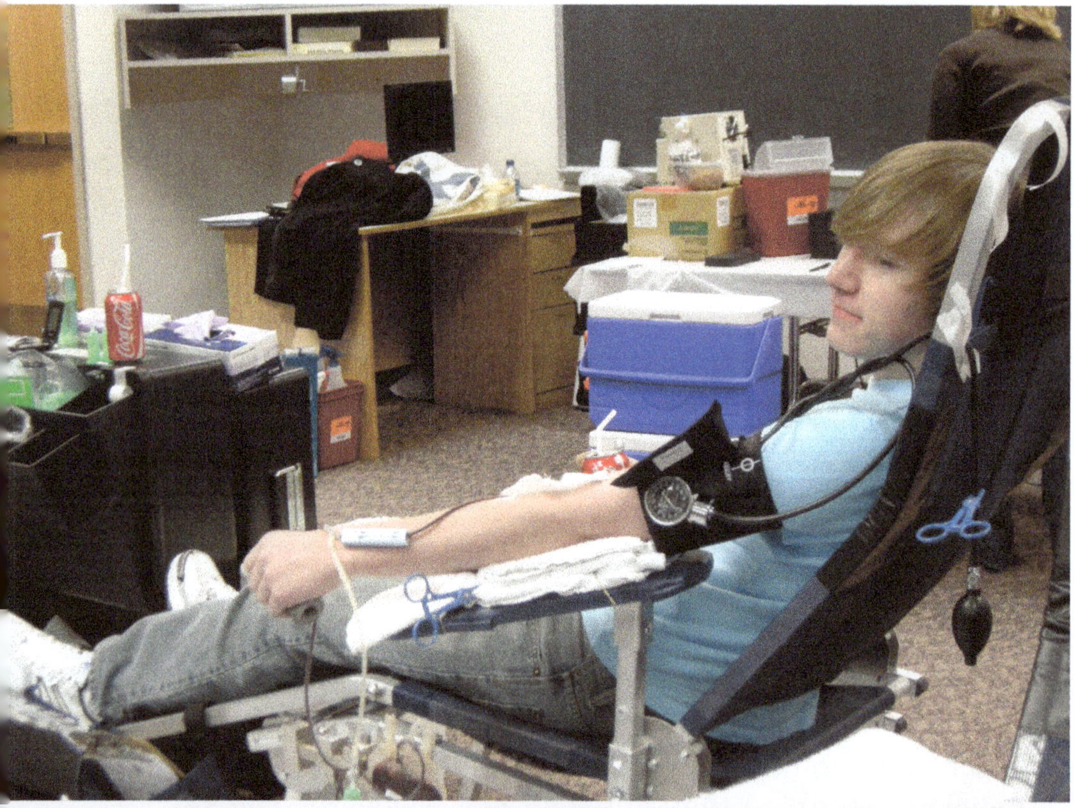

According to the American Red Cross, "almost 20 percent of the millions of donations made each year come from high school and college blood drives."

program for developing neighborhoods. There are also care homes for mature adults who may be interested in lessons regarding nutritional needs, public and personal safety, and staying physically active.

BUILD YOUR TEAM

Once you have determined your mission, it's time to recruit others who will be equally as dedicated. The first group you approach should be your school board and faculty. By reaching out to your guidance counselors, teachers, and administrative staff, they can work with you to gather schoolwide support. The faculty can help you design a top-notch project from top to bottom using online and in-print tools, resources, and support. They can also enlist the help of an entire class or student body.

When in search of impassioned volunteers, talk to your teacher or guidance counselor first. He or she will have a surefire way of finding the right people to help you achieve your project goals.

When enlisting the help of your peers, consider showing them the heart of the issue first. Let them see what you saw, feel

PASS "GO" AND COLLECT GRANT MONEY

Implementing a service-learning project takes money. There's the cost of supplies, transportation to and from the community center, and utilities (gas and electricity), which can take a serious slice out of any donated funds. This is when grant money can keep your project going.

As a service-learning project leader, you may be called upon to apply for a grant in order to keep the project running. The State Farm Youth Advisory Board (YAB) is one of several funding groups who help "passionate, engaged individuals who want to 'change the world'." Since 2006, its thirty-member board of American and Canadian high school, community college, and Ivy League university students have awarded more than $28.6 million to exceptional, student-driven service-learning projects. Each year, YAB divides $5 million among youth-driven, sustainable projects that directly engage K–12 students. Eligibility includes public K–12 and charter schools, colleges and universities, governmental organizations, and nonprofit organizations in the United States and in the Canadian provinces of Alberta, New Brunswick, and Ontario.

When students apply for grants, they can list their projects under one of these categories: Arts and Culture, Access to Higher Education/Closing the Achievement Gap, and Financial Literacy (and Economic Inclusion). The areas of health and safety are also included with Community Safety and Natural Disaster Preparedness. These categories are aimed at keeping the community in good working order, especially in light of recent acts of violence, natural disasters, and social issues.

Ready to get started with an international health and safety project? Your idea may be creative enough to win grant money that will cover travel, supplies, and special event expenses.

Health and Wellness, the third health and safety category, addresses topics such as nutritional imbalances, mental illness, obesity rates, sexual assaults, and sexually transmitted infections. The last category is Environmental Responsibility, which awards projects that improve local and global environments while addressing matters such as climate change, environmental education, wildlife conservation, and land preservation.

It is recommended that programs that are vying for the grant should have the guidance of an adult coordinator. But keep in mind that the responsibility of creating, planning, writing, and applying falls on the shoulders of the students. This makes it a youth-driven program that directly impacts public school curriculum and expands to states and provinces.

what you felt, and hear what you heard. In other words, they will need to experience the same emotional response you did in order to win their hearts and their help. Follow up with a detailed description of what service learning really is. Let them know it's a unique educational movement that is different from the usual volunteering, internship, or community service activity. And while these are great in their own right, a service-learning activity comes with very specific benefits. The time investment is not short-term, and neither are the results. Communities will feel the ripple effect of your help for years to come. Your peers, should they choose to join you, will gain first-hand knowledge in the subjects they're studying. They'll sharpen their critical-thinking, problem-solving, and communication skills, all the while leap-frogging over obstacles. Nothing will be too difficult for your team.

As the service-learning initiative is underway, teachers will monitor the quality, participation, and reflection process to make sure everyone is doing his or her part to reach the desired result. And don't forget to include parents. They are your biggest fans and may be eager to help you brainstorm ideas, fundraise, collect supplies, research grants, make fliers, build props, spread the word, and get you and your classmates from one place to the next. Parent-teacher groups, such as a Parent-Teacher Association (PTA), Parent-Teacher Organization (PTO), or Parent-Teacher-Student Association (PTSA), usually welcome students who have an exciting announcement to make. In fact, they have been known to schedule time at meetings for students to spread the word about their cause and solicit help from group members.

FINE-TUNE THE DETAILS

As the mastermind behind your service-learning project, you and your team will need to create a master plan. It should include a defined end-goal and a timeline of events. Don't forget to include periods of reflection throughout the duration of the project. Students should be able to express their thoughts and feelings privately and within the group. This is a key element that will bring meaning to the experience. Be sure to circulate the master plan among your team and coordinate with all supporters and community member early on in the process.

GENERATE A BUZZ

Now it's time to spread the word about your exciting new project. Social media posts, videos, fliers, posters, and online and in-print press releases will generate a buzz about your efforts. Tell everyone what you're doing whenever you can—the growth and success of your project may depend on attention from the general public. You'll want to "fill the seats" in your meetings, events, and fundraisers, and this kind of marketing will help you do just that. Make sure to include the who, what, when, where, why, and how. Also make sure to fill everyone in on the end goal, the potential for your project's growth, and the positive impact it will have on

Service-learning projects rely on social media campaigns and podcasts to reach a global audience. If you're tech savvy, lend your talents and make a difference in the lives of others.

the community. You never know who will be encouraged to join you, make a donation, or start a similar health and safety project of their own. If you are connecting with a large group or a number of media outlets, you may want to appoint a public relations person who is a good speaker and can accurately share all of the details of your project and provide your contact information.

MEETING STANDARDS FOR HIGH QUALITY SERVICE-LEARNING ADVENTURES

The National Youth Leadership Council (NYLC) drew upon two decades of service-learning wisdom, practice, and counsel to create eight K–12 Service-Learning Standards for Quality Practice. These benchmarks guarantee that students, teachers, school administrators, community members, organizational staff, and policymakers enjoy a high-quality service-learning experience. Below are the eight Standards for Quality Practice as noted on nylc.org:

Meaningful Service Service-learning actively engages participants in meaningful and personally relevant service activities.

Link to Curriculum Service learning is intentionally used as an instructional strategy to meet learning goals and/or content standards.

Reflection Service learning incorporates multiple challenging reflection activities that are ongoing and that prompt deep thinking and analysis about oneself and one's relationship to society.

Diversity Service learning promotes understanding of diversity and mutual respect among all participants.

(continued on the next page)

(continued from the previous page)

Youth Voice Service learning provides youth with a strong voice in planning, implementing, and evaluating service-learning experiences with guidance from adults.

Partnerships Service-learning partnerships are collaborative, mutually beneficial, and address community needs.

Progress Monitoring Service learning engages participants in an ongoing process to assess the quality of implementation and progress toward meeting specified goals, and uses results for improvement and sustainability.

Duration and Intensity Service learning has sufficient duration and intensity to address community needs and meet specified outcomes.

ENJOY THE MOMENTS OF YOUR SERVICE LEARNING PROJECT

With all of the responsibilities you have within your service-learning initiative, make sure to keep one thing in mind: Your efforts may mean the world to one person. That one person may then share with others the impact you've made. He or she may then get involved with a service project of his or her own. And so the ripple effect continues. Sure, things will get busy. You'll have challenges to face, but you'll have help. Lean on your peers, your school or organization's faculty, and your parents for support. They all want to see you succeed. Stay focused, maintain a can-do attitude, and you will have great success for the duration of your commitment. After all, there is no failure in giving to others.

WRAP IT ALL UP

You will need to put together a final demonstration of the educational impact of the project. This can be a picnic, presentation, or theatrical performance. Share evidence of your project's accomplishments with the broader community (policymakers and education leaders) to deepen understanding and ensure high-quality practices are used. Just make sure to document all of your work. A log that includes every step you've taken along the way, from the early brainstorming to the presentation, will be very handy. Save all of your meeting notes, communications with others, completed grant forms, and marketing materials in one place for future reference. You never know—this could come in handy should you decide to expand your project or share the formula with other schools and organizations.

Finally, it's time to celebrate! One of the most important aspects of any service-learning initiative is publicly applauding the hard work of your team, advising faculty, parents, sponsors, and community members. A celebration is a good way to say thank you and wrap it all up.

Enhance the beauty—and functionality—of green spaces by planting trees. Volunteers can research the best tree variety for the location as well as dig, plant, and celebrate at a dedication ceremony.

You could throw a pizza party, host a day in the park, or plan a victory lap after a marathon. Just make sure to keep the fun coming and enjoy the journey of achieving your service-learning goal.

A FEW FINAL WORDS

Service-learning youth represent an amazing component to the health and productivity of our communities and our future. Each year, thousands of service-learning projects contribute millions of hours to communities across the United States, Canada, and the globe. We honor the role of youth participants as they provide their time, energy, and passion to ensure the health and safety of those around them. Their impact has been great, and the future is bright for those who want to continue the service-learning tradition. Join the movement today, and become a part of the change in your community. Inspire your classmates, neighbors, friends, and family with your passion and leadership. Empower others to take the opportunity to create a ripple effect of positivity and lasting change in your community by creating or joining a service-learning project today.

GLOSSARY

agriculture The science or practice of cultivating the earth, growing crops, and raising livestock.

agriculture mechanics The knowledge and skills associated with agricultural construction, equipment, machinery repair, maintenance, operation, and equipment.

alliance A formal agreement between two or more individuals or groups to reach a common goal.

audit A formal examination and review of one's personal or professional banking accounts or financial situation.

clinical rotations An unpaid internship in which a medical practitioner in training is paired with a clinical instructor.

critical thinking Rational consideration that is clear, open-minded, and based on evidence.

e-waste Short for electronic waste, this term describes outdated appliances or electronics such as computers, cell phones, and microwaves.

fitness screenings A series of exercises designed to measure one's level of physical fitness.

grant A form of financial aid that is given by a government body or organization that does not need to be repaid.

health screening Medical tests provided by doctors, health clinics, and community centers used to expose potentially life-threatening diseases before symptoms appear in a patient.

horticulture The art, science, business, and technology of a garden, orchard, or nursery.

internship A capstone experience at the end of one's formal education program.

interpersonal skills Social skills that are used to communicate and interact with an individual or group.

musculoskeletal disorders Injuries to the muscles, nerves, cartilage, tendons, joints, and spinal discs.

neurological disorders Diseases of the brain, spine, and the connecting nerves.

pedagogy The art or science of educating others.

physical therapy Medical treatment that uses massage, heat, and exercise to treat physical injury, disease, or disfigurement.

soil infiltration The descending entry of water into the soil.

sustainability The ability to sustain despite internal and external challenges.

ultrasound A high-frequency sound wave beyond audible range that is used to create an image of various organs within the body.

FOR MORE INFORMATION

Campus Compact
45 Temple Place
Boston, MA 02111
(617) 357-1881
Website: http://www.compact.org
Campus Compact is a national association of over six million students who are dedicated to fulfilling civic purposes through service learning. Its National Service-Learning Clearinghouse offers how-to tips on starting service-learning projects and provides resources, fact sheets, and hot topics.

Canadian Alliance for Community Service-Learning (CACSL)
2128 Dunton Tower
Carleton University
1125 Colonel By Drive
Ottawa, ON K1S 5B6
Canada
(613) 520-2600, ext. 8241
Website: http://www.communityservicelearning.ca
The CACSL is a national alliance that provides resources and support to Canadian students, educators, and community members who are active in community service-learning projects.

Corporation for National and Community Service
1201 New York Avenue NW
Washington, DC 20525
(202) 606-5000
Website: http://www.nationalservice.gov

Chartered by Congress in 1993, the Corporation for National Service provides opportunities to service-oriented Americans of all ages and backgrounds. Learn and Serve America, one of its grant programs, supports service-learning programs that engage almost one million students.

Learn and Serve America (LSA)
1201 New York Avenue NW
Washington, DC 20525
(800) 833-3722
Website: http://www.learnandserve.gov
Created under the National and Community Service Act of 1990, LSA allocates grants for service-learning projects.

National FFA Organization
P.O. Box 68960
6060 FFA Drive
Indianapolis, IN 46268
(317) 802-6060
Website: http://www.ffa.org
Founded by young farmers in 1928, Future Farmers of America (FFA) was designed to prepare future generations for the challenges of feeding a growing population. Today, the National FFA Organization helps members to explore a broad array of careers in biology, chemistry, engineering, and business.

National Service Learning Resource Center
ETR Associates

4 Carbonero Way
Scotts Valley, CA 95066
(831) 438-4060
Website: http://www.etr.org
As an arm of the Corporation for National and Community Service, the National Service Learning Resource Center is a hub for shared training. It connects teachers and trainers to grant opportunities, while providing resources for environmental service projects.

National Society for Experiential Education (NSEE)
c/o Talley Management Group, Inc.
19 Mantua Road
Mt. Royal, NJ 08061
(856) 423-3427
Website: http://www.nsee.org/
Founded in 1971, NSEE offers educators, businesses, and community leaders resources to develop and improve their experiential education programs in the United States.

National Youth Leadership Council (NYLC)
1667 Snelling Avenue North, Suite D300
St. Paul, MN 55108
(651) 631-3672
Website: http://www.nylc.org
NYLC is a nonprofit organization that promotes service-learning initiatives among young people, educators, and communities in the United States and Canada. They have a menu of programs, consulting services,

training opportunities, and publications to further the success of such initiatives.

Youth Service America (YSA)
1101 15th Street NW, Suite 200
Washington, DC 20005
(202) 296-2992
Website: http://www.ysa.org
YSA provides free resources for high-quality, high-impact service and service-learning projects. It sponsors Global Youth Service Day each year, a day of celebrating service-learning students from all over the world.

WEBSITES

Because of the changing nature of Internet links, Rosen Publishing has developed an online list of websites related to the subject of this book. This site is updated regularly. Please use this link to access the list:

http://www.rosenlinks.com/SLFT/Heal

FOR FURTHER READING

Appleman, Dan. *Developing Teen Leadership: A Practical Guide for Youth Group Advisors, Teachers and Parents.* San Jose, CA: Desaware Publishing, 2011.

Bringle, Robert G., Julie A. Hatcher, Steven G. Jones, eds. *International Service Learning: Conceptual Frameworks and Research.* Sterling, VA: Stylus Publishing, LLC, 2010.

Butin, Dan W. *Service-Learning in Theory and Practice: The Future of Community Engagement in Higher Education.* New York, NY: Palgrave Macmillan, 2010.

Cress, Christine M., Peter J. Collier, and Vicki L. Reitenauer. *Learning Through Serving: A Student Guidebook for Service-Learning and Civic Engagement Across Academic Disciplines and Cultural Communities.* Sterling, VA: Stylus Publishing, LLC, 2013.

Covey, Stephen R. *The Leader in Me: How Schools and Parents Around the World Are Inspiring Greatness, One Child at a Time.* New York, NY: Free Press, 2009.

Jones, Stephen W. *Intercultural Development in Global Service-Learning.* North Charleston, SC: CreateSpace Independent Publishing Platform, 2013.

Kavaloski, Vincent and Jane Hammatt Kavaloski. *Tough Minds and Tender Hearts: Building Martin Luther King's "Beloved Community" Through Service-Learning.* St. Paul, MN: National Youth Leadership Council, 2011.

Lake, Vickie E., and Ithel Jones. *Service Learning in the PreK–3 Classroom: The What, Why, and How-To*

Guide for Every Teacher. Minneapolis, MN: Free Spirit Publishing, Inc., 2012.

Lewis, Barbara A. *The Kid's Guide to Service Projects: Over 500 Service Ideas for Young People Who Want to Make a Difference.* Minneapolis, MN: Free Spirit Publishing, Inc., 2009.

MacGregor, Mariam G. *Building Everyday Leadership in All Kids: An Elementary Curriculum to Promote Attitudes and Actions for Respect and Success.* Minneapolis, MN: Free Spirit Publishing, Inc., 2013.

Marquet, David. *Turn the Ship Around!: A True Story of Turning Followers into Leaders.* New York, NY: Penguin Group, 2013.

Miller, Marybeth P., and James D. Nendel. *Service-Learning In Physical Education And Other Related Professions: A Global Perspective.* Sudbury, MA: Jones & Bartlett Learning, 2010.

Newton, Fred B., and Steven C. Ender. *Students Helping Students: A Guide for Peer Educators on College Campuses.* San Francisco, CA: John Wiley & Sons, Inc., 2010.

The Seed Leadership Project. *Decisions Shape Destiny: Wisdom for Teens and Young Adults.* North Charleston, SC: CreateSpace Independent Publishing Platform, 2013.

Sinek, Simon. *Start with Why: How Great Leaders Inspire Everyone to Take Action.* New York, NY: Penguin Group, 2009.

Sturt, David. *Great Work: How to Make a Difference People Love.* Salt Lake City, UT: O. C. Tanner Company, 2013.

Sundem, Garth. *Real Kids, Real Stories, Real Change: Courageous Actions Around the World.* Minneapolis, MN: Free Spirit Publishing, Inc., 2010.

Thelen, Tom. *Teen Leadership Revolution: How Ordinary Teens Become Extraordinary Leaders.* Lowell, MI: Character Programs, 2012.

Xing, Jun, ed. *Service-Learning in Asia: Curricular Models and Practices.* Aberdeen, Hong Kong: Hong Kong University Press, 2009.

BIBLIOGRAPHY

Bankston, Carl L., III. "Modern Orthodoxies." The John Williams Pope Center, 2011. Retrieved February 7, 2014 (http://www.popecenter.org/commentaries/article.html?id=2537).

Callahan, Laurie. "Skillful Hands, Caring Hearts." Retrieved March 12, 2014 (http://www.marymount.edu/newsEvents/MUToday/issue74/hands.aspx).

Center for Civic Engagement. "Service Learning: Ivy Tech Community College-Bloomington." 2012. Retrieved March 1, 2014 (http://www.ivytech.edu/bloomington/civicengagement/Service_Learning_Brochure_web.pdf).

Cervone, Barbara. "Learning by Heart: Giving Back at Quest Early College High School." WKCD: What Kids Can Do. Retrieved March 3, 2014 (http://www.howyouthlearn.org/SEL_closeup_QECHS.html#sthash.colb4rui.dpuf).

Distraction.gov. "What Is Distracted Driving?" Retrieved July 15, 2014 (http://www.distraction.gov/content/get-the-facts/facts-and-statistics.html).

Environmental Protection Agency. "Learning by Doing: Students Take Greening to the Community, Edition 3."2011. Retrieved March 4, 2014 (http://www.epa.gov/osw/education/pdfs/svclearn.pdf).

Flinn, Andrew. "Ridgemont FFA Working to Combat Hunger." KentonToday.com, 2013. Retrieved March 2, 2014 (http://wktn.com/ag-news/72992#sthash.cQ4TSwhk.dpuf).

The Florida Department of Education and Florida Campus Compact. "Standards for Service-Learning in Florida: A Guide for Creating and Sustaining Quality Practice." Retrieved March 1, 2014 (http://www.fsu.edu/~flserve/resources/SL%20Standards%20for%20SL%20in%20FL.pdf).

Frasco, Jenny. "Service Learning-Celebration Concept." Grand Valley State University. Retrieved February 7, 2014 (http://learningtogive.org/papers/paper240.html).

International Service Learning. "About ISL." Retrieved March 13, 2014 (http://www.islonline.org/about).

Ivy Tech Community College Bloomington News. "Civic Engagement Awards ceremony at Ivy Tech to honor volunteers, celebrate economic impact." April 9, 2013. Retrieved March 13, 2014 (http://ivytechbloomington.wordpress.com/2013/04/09/civic-engagement-awards-ceremony-at-ivy-tech-to-honor-volunteers-celebrate-economic-impact).

Kaye, C.B. *The Complete Guide to Service Learning: Proven, Practical Ways to Engage Students in Civic Responsibility, Academic Curriculum, & Social Action.* Minneapolis, MN: Free Spirit Publishing, Inc., 2010.

Milwaukee Public Schools. "Student-Learning: An Implementation Guide for High School Teachers." 2013. Retrieved March 3, 2014 (http://www5.milwaukee.k12.wi.us/dept/teamup/files/2013/01/Revised-2013-14_-MPS_Service).

National FFA Organization. "FFA: Food For All grants help fight hunger." 2013. Retrieved March 2, 2014 (http://nationalffa.wordpress.com/2013/04/09/ffa-food-for-all-grants-help-fight-hunger/).

National FFA Organization. "FFA Membership Explodes to 579,678 Students." 2013. Retrieved March 2, 2014 (http://nationalffa.wordpress.com/2013/09/30/ffa-membership-explodes-to-579678-students).

National Youth Leadership Council. "Blankets, Babies, and HIV/AIDS Awareness." Retrieved March 3, 2014 (http://www.nylc.org/resources/projects/blankets-babies-and-hivaids-awareness).

National Youth Leadership Council. "Giving Safety Wings." 2013. Retrieved March 3, 2014 (http://www.nylc.org/resources/projects/giving-safety-wings).

National Youth Leadership Council. "K–12 Service-Learning Standards for Quality Practice." Retrieved March 2, 2014 (http://www.nylc.org/sites/nylc.org/files/files/Standards_Oct2009-web.pdf).

National Youth Leadership Council. "Project Ignition Grants Available to High School Students to Improve Teen Driving." 2013. Retrieved February 6, 2014 (http://www.nylc.org/news/project-ignition-grants-available-high-school-students-improve-teen-driving).

National Youth Leadership Council. "Safety on the Bus." Retrieved March 3, 2014 (http://www.nylc.org/resources/projects/safety-bus).

Nutrients for Life. "Winners of the Ohio FFA 'Helping Communities Grow' Program." 2013. Retrieved February 17, 2014 (https://www.nutrientsforlife

.org/release/winners-ohio-ffa-%E2%80%9Chelping-communities-grow%E2%80%9D-program).

1000 New Gardens Montana. "Coffee 2 Compost In a Nutshell." Retrieved March 11, 2014 (http://1000newgardens.ning.com/page/coffee-2-compost-in-a-nutshell).

Ridgemont Local Schools. "Back Pack Buddies." 2014. Retrieved March 2, 2014 (http://www.ridgemont.k12.oh.us/BackPackBuddies.aspx).

Roberts, Pamela. "The Bus Bully Project." Responsive Classroom, 2002. Retrieved March 16, 2014 (http://www.responsiveclassroom.org/article/bus-bully-project).

Rutgers: Center for Global Education. "Rutgers ISL Programs 2014." 2014. Retrieved March 13, 2014 (http://studyabroad.rutgers.edu/index.cfm?FuseAction=Abroad).

Stanton, Timothy K., Dwight E. Giles, Jr., and Nadinne I. Cruz. *Service Learning.* Engergize, Inc. Retrieved February 7, 2014 (http://www.energizeinc.com/art/aser.html).

Stubbs, Emily. "Helping Communities Grow Spotlight: Ridgemont FFA." Nutrients for Life Foundation, 2012. Retrieved February 17, 2014 (http://blog.nutrientsforlife.org/2012/07/ffa-helping-communities-grow-spotlight-ridgemont-ffa).

UN News Center. "World Population Projected to Reach 9.6 Billion by 2050—UN report." 2013. Retrieved March 16, 2014 (http://www.un.org/apps/news/story.asp?NewsID=45165#.UyYx2Gnn_IU).

The University of British Columbia. "Connecting at Christmas." Retrieved March 17, 2014 (http://www.ubc.ca/okanagan/students/cslprogram/pastprojects/christmas.html).

Wick, Benjamin. "Service Learning on a Global Scale | Safe Streets, Healthy Kids Week 4." Radio Milwaukee, 2011. Retrieved March 13, 2014 (http://www.radiomilwaukee.org/initiatives/safe-streets-healthy-kids/service-learning-global-scale-safe-streets-healthy-kids-week-4#sthash.QqtnpOOv.dpuf).

INDEX

ABOUT THE AUTHOR

Erin Staley's work ranges from nonfiction books (Rosen Publishing) to online and in-print content for North American businesses and nonprofit organizations.

PHOTO CREDITS

Cover Leon Halip/NHLI/Getty Images; p. 3 bymandesigns/Shutterstock.com; p. 5 Geoffrey Kuchera/Shutterstock.com; p. 7 Fuzzbones/Shutterstock.com; pp. 8–9 David Sacks/The Image Bank/Getty Images; p. 10 © The Fresno Bee/ZUMA Press; p. 11 Creatas Images/Thinkstock; p. 13 Pawel Gaul/E+/Getty Images; p. 16 Hulton Archive/Getty Images; p. 19 © iStockphoto.com/eurobanks; p. 20 Lori Adamski Peek/The Image Bank/Getty Images; p. 22 Kevin Dodge/Blend Images/Getty Images; p. 24 kristian sekulic/E+/Getty Images; p. 26 Jesse A Wanskasmith/First Light/Getty Images; p. 29 iStockphoto.com/Yvan Dubé; p. 31 (top) Flashon Studio/Shutterstock.com; pp. 31 (bottom), 38, 40 (bottom), 44 © AP Images; p. 34 John Coletti/The Image Bank/Getty Images; p. 35 Ron Sherman/The Image Bank/Getty Images; 40 (top) Antonio Guillem/Shutterstock.com; pp. 46–47, 55 Hero Images/Getty Images; p. 50 Warren Diggles Photography/Moment/Getty Images; 51 Tom Wang/Shutterstock.com; p. 52 Education Images/Universal Images Group/Getty Images; p. 53 Blend Images/Ariel Skelley/Vetta/Getty Images; p. 58 Till Jacket/Photononstop/Getty Images; p. 62 Blend Images/KidStock/Brand X Pictures/Getty Images; cover and interior pages background textures and patterns vector illustration/Shutterstock.com, Apostrophe/Shutterstock.com, nattanan726/Shutterstock.com, Yulia Glam/Shutterstock.com; back cover silhouette Pavel L Photo and Video/Shutterstock.com.

Designer: Michael Moy; Photo Researcher: Karen Huang